A Note to Parents and Caregivers:

Read-it! Readers are for children who are just starting on the amazing road to reading. These beautiful books support both the acquisition of reading skills and the love of books.

The RED LEVEL presents familiar topics using common words and repeating sentence patterns.
The BLUE LEVEL presents new ideas using a larger vocabulary and varied sentence structure.
The YELLOW LEVEL presents more challenging ideas, a broad vocabulary, and wide variety in sentence structure.

When sharing a book with your child, read in short stretches, pausing often to talk about the pictures. Have your child turn the pages and point to the pictures and familiar words. And be sure to reread favorite stories or parts of stories.

There is no right or wrong way to share books with children. Find time to read with your child, and pass on the legacy of literacy.

Adria F. Klein, Ph.D.
Professor Emeritus
California State University
San Bernardino, California

First American edition published in 2003 by
Picture Window Books
5115 Excelsior Boulevard
Suite 232
Minneapolis, MN 55416
1-877-845-8392
www.picturewindowbooks.com

First published in Great Britain by Franklin Watts, 96 Leonard Street, London, EC2A 4XD
Text © Ann Bryant 2000
Illustration © Claire Henley 2000

Printed in the United States of America.

Library of Congress Cataloging-in-Publication Data
Bryant, Ann.
  Jack's party / written by Ann Bryant ; illustrated by Claire Henley.—1st American ed.
    p. cm. — (Read-it! readers)
  Summary: At his birthday party, Jack tries to stop a game that his guests want to play
because he knows they won't like the prize—or does he?
  ISBN 1-4048-0060-3
  [1. Birthdays—Fiction. 2. Parties—Fiction.] I. Henley, Claire, ill. II. Title. III. Series.
  PZ7.B8298 Jac 2003
  [E]—dc21   2002074936

PICTURE WINDOW BOOKS
Minneapolis, Minnesota

Read-it! Readers
Blue Level

Jack's Party

Written by Ann Bryant

Illustrated by Claire Henley

Reading Advisors:
Adria F. Klein, Ph.D.
Professor Emeritus, California State University
San Bernardino, California

Ruth Thomas
Durham Public Schools
Durham, North Carolina

R. Ernice Bookout
Durham Public Schools
Durham, North Carolina

Picture Window Books
Minneapolis, Minnesota

It was Jack's birthday party and he was having a great time, until . . .

Amy tripped over her shoelace. Jack heard her mumble, "I hate painting faces!"

"Me too!" everyone agreed.

Jack began to worry.

Jack's mom came back
from the kitchen.

"Who wants to play Pass the Present?" she asked.

Jack frowned.
He knew what was
inside the present.

"I'm not playing," he said.

The music started.
The present went around
the circle.

The music stopped.
Tom ripped off the first layer
of paper.

15

"Let's play musical chairs," said Jack.

"Pass the Present is for babies."

"No!" everyone shouted.

"We want Pass the Present!"

Jean ripped off another
layer of paper.

Jack pressed the stop
button on the CD player.

"Oh no, it's broken! Let's watch a video," Jack said.

Jack's mom pressed the play button again.

Molly ripped off the next
layer of paper.

Josh ripped off the one
after that.

Jack held his breath.

Everyone watched as Amy ripped off the last layer.

"Great, it's face paints!"
shouted Amy.

"I thought you said you hated painting faces," said Jack.

"No, I said I hate **tying laces**," said Amy.

30

"Painting faces is great!"

Red Level

The Best Snowman, by Margaret Nash 1-4048-0048-4
Bill's Baggy Pants, by Susan Gates 1-4048-0050-6
Cleo and Leo, by Anne Cassidy 1-4048-0049-2
Felix on the Move, by Maeve Friel 1-4048-0055-7
Jasper and Jess, by Anne Cassidy 1-4048-0061-1
The Lazy Scarecrow, by Jillian Powell 1-4048-0062-X
Little Joe's Big Race, by Andy Blackford 1-4048-0063-8
The Little Star, by Deborah Nash 1-4048-0065-4
The Naughty Puppy, by Jillian Powell 1-4048-0067-0
Selfish Sophie, by Damian Kelleher 1-4048-0069-7

Blue Level

The Bossy Rooster, by Margaret Nash 1-4048-0051-4
Jack's Party, by Ann Bryant 1-4048-0060-3
Little Red Riding Hood, by Maggie Moore 1-4048-0064-6
Recycled!, by Jillian Powell 1-4048-0068-9
The Sassy Monkey, by Anne Cassidy 1-4048-0058-1
The Three Little Pigs, by Maggie Moore 1-4048-0071-9

Yellow Level

Cinderella, by Barrie Wade 1-4048-0052-2
The Crying Princess, by Anne Cassidy 1-4048-0053-0
Eight Enormous Elephants, by Penny Dolan 1-4048-0054-9
Freddie's Fears, by Hilary Robinson 1-4048-0056-5
Goldilocks and the Three Bears, by Barrie Wade 1-4048-0057-3
Mary and the Fairy, by Penny Dolan 1-4048-0066-2
Jack and the Beanstalk, by Maggie Moore 1-4048-0059-X
The Three Billy Goats Gruff, by Barrie Wade 1-4048-0070-0